W9-AVA-682

BL 2.1

For Sebastian

—E.C.

Clarion Books • a Houghton Mifflin Company imprint • 215 Park Avenue South, New York, NY 10003 • Text and illustrations copyright © 1996 by Eileen Christelow • Illustrations executed in gouache and pen and ink on Lanaquarelle hot-press watercolor paper • Text is 15/21-point Century Oldstyle • All rights reserved. • For information about permission to reproduce selections from this book, write to Permissions, Houghton Mifflin Company, 215 Park Avenue South, New York, NY 10003. • For information about this and other Houghton Mifflin trade and reference books and multimedia products, visit The Bookstore at Houghton Mifflin on the World Wide Web at (http://www.hmco.com/trade/). • Printed in the USA • **Library of Congress Cataloging-in-Publication Data** • Christelow, Eileen. • Five little monkeys with nothing to do / written and illustrated by Eileen Christelow. • p.   cm. • Summary: Five little monkeys are bored, but their mother has them clean up the house for Grandma Bessie's visit. • ISBN 0-395-75830-0 • [1. Monkeys—Fiction.   2. House cleaning—Fiction.]   I. Title. PZ7.C4523Fl   1996   [E]—dc20 • 95-25873 CIP AC • HOR 10 9 8 7 6 5 4 3 2 1

Five Little Monkeys With Nothing To Do

Written and Illustrated by **Eileen Christelow**

Clarion Books/New York

It is summer. There is no school.
Five little monkeys tell their mama,
"We're bored. There is nothing to do!"
   "Oh yes there is," says Mama.
"Grandma Bessie is coming for lunch,
and the house must be neat and clean.

"So . . . you can pick up your room."

9

Five little monkeys pick up and pick up and pick up . . .

. . . until everything is put away.

12

"Good job!" says Mama.
"But we're bored again,"
say five little monkeys.
"There is nothing to do!"
"Oh yes there is," says Mama.
"You can scrub the bathroom.
The house must be neat and clean
for Grandma Bessie."

So five little monkeys scrub and scrub
and scrub until the bathroom shines.

"Good job!" says Mama.
"But we're bored again,"
say five little monkeys.
"There is nothing to do!"
"Oh yes there is," says Mama.
"You can beat the dirt out of these rugs.
The house must be neat and clean
for Grandma Bessie."

Five little monkeys beat and beat and beat the rugs until there is not a speck of dirt left.

"Good job!" says Mama.
"But we're bored again," say five little monkeys.
"There is nothing to do!"

"Oh yes there is," says Mama.
"You can pick some berries down by the swamp.
Grandma Bessie loves berries for dessert."

Five little monkeys run down
to the muddy, muddy swamp.

They pick and pick and pick berries
until Mama calls, "It's time to come home!"

Five little monkeys run inside
while Mama picks flowers.
    "Put the berries in the kitchen,"
calls Mama. "Wash your faces
and put on clean clothes."

Five little monkeys wash their faces . . .

. . . and they put on clean clothes.
"Grandma Bessie is here!" calls Mama.

Five little monkeys race outside.

They hug and kiss Grandma Bessie.
"We've been busy all day!" they say.
"We cleaned the house and picked berries
just for you!"

"I love berries," says Grandma Bessie.
"And I love a clean house, too!"

They all go inside.

"Oh my!" says Grandma Bessie.
"Oh dear!" says Mama.
"Oh no!" say five little monkeys.
"Who messed up our nice, clean house?"

"I can't imagine," says Mama.
"But whoever did has plenty to do!"